So DRAMATIC!

My sincere thanks to the NLD authors for allowing their books to be adapted for this book:

John Parsons, Christchurch, New Zealand

Stella Santa Cruz, Melbourne, Australia

Dear Reader

While watching great dramatic performances, I enjoy observing actors who manage to skilfully transform themselves into their character and deliver a performance that's believable and entertaining. Sometimes, actors are so good that you almost feel like you have been transported to the time and place where the performance is set.

> **"ALL THE WORLD'S A STAGE AND ALL THE MEN AND WOMEN MERELY PLAYERS ..."**
>
> WILLIAM SHAKESPEARE

All great dramatic actors need well-written scripts and, in Chapters 4–7, you'll get some practical guidance on how to write an entertaining comedy script, a script for a TV advertisement, a musical comedy script and an adaptation of a book for a stage performance.

Have fun using these ideas to write your own scripts!

Sharon Parsons

Contents

So DRAMATIC!

1 The Early History of Drama

What Is Drama?

The word "drama" has an ancient Greek origin. It originally meant "deed" or "action", but came to refer to deeds and actions presented in a theatrical setting.

Ancient Greek Drama

In ancient Greece, drama was an important way for actors (usually male) to express their impressions of people in society, via three main dramatic genres: comedy, tragedy and satyr plays.

Greek Comedies

Ancient Greek comedies could be likened to modern stand-up comedies. They were plays written and performed to mock the vanity and foolishness of people in power.

Greek Tragedy

In plays of tragedy, the ancient Greeks depicted themes that are still important in dramatic performances today. Tragedies explore how people relate to one another in all kinds of situations, and may involve a range of emotions, such as love, loss, happiness, sadness and excitement. Tragedies almost always have sad endings, and today people believe that this is so the audience leaves the play feeling that their own lives are good in comparison to the suffering they have seen on stage.

Greek Satyr

In Greek mythology, a satyr is a mischievous being that is half man and half goat. Ancient Greek satyr plays were short enough to be performed in between the acts of a tragedy dramatic performance. They usually made fun of the characters who were most affected by unfortunate events in the tragedy plays. Some of today's comedies are called "satires", a word derived from the same name.

Drama Today

Just as the ancient Greeks expressed themselves through drama all those years ago, dramatic performers today continue this artistic tradition. The art form of drama provides all cultures with a powerful medium through which to express themselves. Whether dramatic performances are improvised or scripted, fiction or based on fact, artistic teams (writers, actors and production crews) use the power of drama to entertain, enlighten, engage and sometimes challenge audiences.

Masks of Drama

A familiar symbol associated with drama is the pair of happy and sad masks, which symbolise two opposite genres – comedy and tragedy.

Happy Mask: This mask represents an ancient Greek muse, Thalia, who was named the "muse of comedy".

Sad Mask: This mask represents Melpomene, the "muse of tragedy".

Thalia (muse of comedy)

Melpomene (muse of tragedy)

Ancient Greek Mythology – Nine Muses

In Greek mythology, the muses are the nine daughters of Mnemosyne, goddess of memory, and Zeus, king of gods. Each of the muses was assigned a certain artistic, literary or scientific skill. The ancient Greeks believed that muses had powers to improve the work of artists and writers, and helped people to feel more joyful.

Terpsichore (muse of dance)

The Nine Muses

Clio (history) *Thalia (comedy)* *Erato (love poetry)* *Euterpe (music)* *Polyhymnia (hymns)* *Calliope (epic poetry)* *Terpsichore (dance)* *Urania (astronomy)* *Melpomene (tragedy)*

2 Shakespeare, So Dramatic

If you asked the question, "Who is history's most famous and talented playwright of very dramatic plays?", most people would answer "William Shakespeare!" More than four hundred years after they were written, Shakespeare's plays still have universal appeal. As well as being performed on stage for hundreds of years, many of Shakespeare's plays have been adapted for movies and television. Some of the most popular Shakespearean plays include *Romeo and Juliet*, *Hamlet* and *A Midsummer Night's Dream*.

William Shakespeare (1564–1616)

the half-timbered house in Stratford-upon-Avon where Shakespeare was born

William Shakespeare

William Shakespeare, who was born in Stratford-upon-Avon in England, lived from 1564 to 1616. He began his career in the theatre as an actor. In collaboration with fellow actors, he formed successful theatre groups and built theatres. It is uncertain how many plays he actually wrote because of poor record keeping at that time, but it is generally accepted that he wrote at least 37 plays – 17 comedies (including *Twelfth Night* and *Much Ado About Nothing*); 10 tragedies (including *Macbeth* and *King Lear*); and 10 histories (including *Henry V* and *Richard III*).

THE BARD

William Shakespeare is often referred to as "the Bard", in recognition of his great contribution to poetry. "Bard" means "poet".

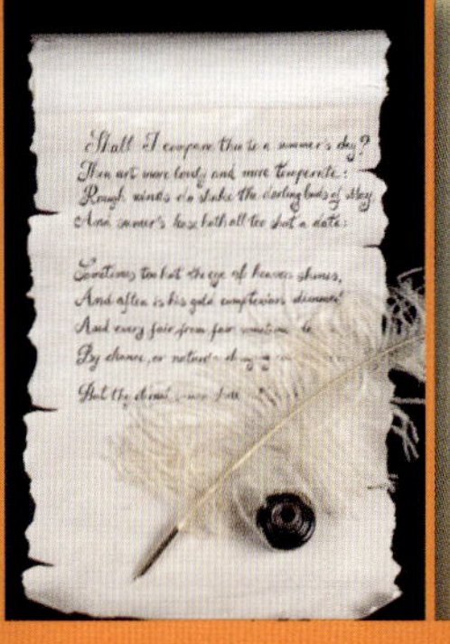

a Shakespearean sonnet

Shakespeare's impressive body of literary works also includes many poems and sonnets (a form of poetry), and records show that he wrote these poetic forms before his plays. He wrote around two plays a year between 1594 and 1611. During his lifetime, Shakespeare's plays were very popular and he became a wealthy man.

William Shakespeare's signature

History

William Shakespeare

William Shakespeare's exact date of birth is unknown. Records show that he was christened on 26 April 1564, which means he would have been born shortly before that date. He died on 23 April 1616. Because of the uncertainty of his birth date, Shakespeare's birthday is officially celebrated on 23 April.

A Famous Shakespearean Quote

All the world's a stage,
And all the men and women merely players;
They have their exits and their entrances;
And one man in his time plays many parts,
His acts being seven ages.

MEANING OF THE QUOTE

This quote is in Act 2 of one of Shakespeare's plays, *As You Like It*, and is often quoted when describing people's roles in life.

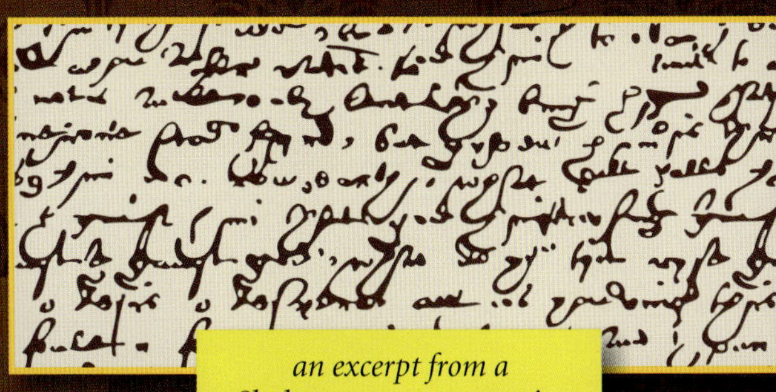

an excerpt from a Shakespearean manuscript

Deciphering Shakespeare's Plays

William Shakespeare lived in England during the reign of Queen Elizabeth I. Elizabethan English, the language of those times, was written and spoken differently to the version of English used today. In Shakespeare's time, most people only had a vocabulary of about 500 words, and there were only 24 letters in the alphabet. There were also different spelling rules and ways of expressing language, which explains why it is not always easy to decipher and understand the language of Shakespeare's works. Many modern scripts of his plays include notes to help today's readers and actors understand the writing. Although most people at the time used only a limited number of words, Shakespeare proved his masterful command of language by inventing over 1 700 new words that would better express his ideas.

Queen Elizabeth I (1533–1603)

Shakespearean Actors on Stage

In Elizabethan times, all professional actors were male, as it was considered inappropriate for women to perform in plays on stage. Adolescent boys were preferred for female characters, because their voices were higher and they were smaller than the adult men, so when they wore make-up and costumes, they looked and sounded somewhat like women. It wasn't until after King Charles II came to the throne in 1660 that this rule in theatre was changed to allow women to perform, too.

If thou can't find the right word, thou shalt just invent it!

Russian actors perform a scene from one of Shakespeare's famous tragedies, Hamlet

a sculptor's impression of Juliet in Verona, Italy

the famous balcony, claimed to be at Juliet's house in Verona, Italy

History

Archaeologists Find Shakespearean Theatre

In 2012, the remains of the Curtain Theatre, where Shakespeare's plays were performed in 1597 and 1598, were uncovered. A site in north-east London was being excavated for development when the chance discovery was made. Shakespearean experts believe that plays such as Romeo and Juliet and Henry V premiered at the Curtain Theatre, which makes this archaeological find even more significant. The developers of the site will now redraw their building plans to preserve the theatre's remains and allow the public to see them.

WHEREFORE ART THOU, JULIET?

Dear Juliet
Verona, Italy

Shakespeare's tragic play *Romeo and Juliet* is also seen as one of his most romantic. Every year, people from all over the world send letters addressed to "Dear Juliet" in Verona, Italy. There, a dedicated group of women respond to millions of love letters.

Shakespeare's Globe Theatre

Shakespeare's theatre company, The Lord Chamberlain's Men, built the Globe Theatre in London, the UK, in 1598–1599. The Globe was a circular, three-storey high, open-air theatre with a seating capacity of about 3 000. It was common for Elizabethan theatres to have this shape. And where were the most expensive seats? Not in the front row or high up in the dress circle, but in the balconies right beside the stage. By sitting in that position, people could see the play up close and also be seen by others!

the entrance to Shakespeare's Globe Theatre in London

Early theatres like the Globe were prone to fire because they were built of flammable materials, like timber frames and thatched roofs. The Globe Theatre burned down in 1613. It was rebuilt by 1614, but was then demolished in 1644. In 1997, a modern-day reproduction of the Globe Theatre was built on the banks of the River Thames in London. Today, this arts centre showcases Shakespeare's unique body of work in stage performances and educational events.

inside the modern-day reproduction of Shakespeare's Globe Theatre

the exterior of Shakespeare's Globe Theatre

World Shakespeare Festival

The World Shakespeare Festival celebrates Shakespeare as a world-renowned playwright across England and around the world. The festival is celebrated from April to November each year.

This major celebration is produced by the Royal Shakespeare Company, Shakespeare's Globe and other arts organisations. Thousands of artists participate in many Shakespearean productions and events around the world, across the UK (including in Shakespeare's birthplace, Stratford-upon-Avon) and online.

Research conducted in the UK has revealed that 50 per cent of the world's students study Shakespeare, which equates to more than 60 million children worldwide.

The World Shakespeare Festival is an opportunity for schools to get involved, too.

banners advertising three of Shakespeare's plays during the World Shakespeare Festival in Stratford-upon-Avon

the Royal Shakespeare Company Theatre, in Stratford-upon-Avon

An engraving from 1877 showing a scene from Shakespeare's tragedy, Macbeth *(Act 4, Scene 2). The boy is asking the question of his mother, Lady Macduff.*

an 1893 edition of Shakespeare's complete collection of works

Perform Shakespeare Anywhere!

Nearly 400 years after his death, the relevant themes and storylines in Shakespeare's plays continue to inspire actors, arts groups and production companies. Shakespeare's works have been translated into many languages, and have been performed almost everywhere, including on lavish stages, at outdoor venues and in movies.

an engraving from 1874 showing a scene from one of Shakespeare's comedies, The Merry Wives of Windsor

actors from the Island Shakespeare Theatre Company, the USA, performing scenes from one of Shakespeare's comedies, Much Ado About Nothing *at an amphitheatre*

scenes from Shakespeare's tragedy, Hamlet, *being performed in Moscow, Russia*

3 Improvisation and Italian Comedy

Improvisation in drama occurs when performances are created and acted out on the spot, without a script or rehearsal. For many actors and performers, improvisation is an exciting challenge that often has moments of hilarity for the performers and the audience.

Improvised Comedy

Commedia dell'arte is a form of improvisational comedy that has its origins in Italy during the sixteenth century. The performers, not the playwrights, usually write the script, but they may improvise parts of the performance according to the audience's response.

Pantalone

We owe some English words to *Commedia dell'arte*, including the word "pants". It comes from one of the *Commedia dell'arte* characters, Pantalone, who wore ankle-length trousers instead of the more common knee-length ones. These trousers came to be called *pantaloons*, after Pantalone. Later, *pantaloons* was shortened to "pants".

Characters from Italian Comedia dell'arte *act out a humorous scene in Russia – Pantalone (right) and a maid servant, Colombina (left)*

a popular Venetian mask worn at Venetian carnivals portraying the Comedia dell'arte *character, Pantalone*

Commedia dell'arte Characters

Students of modern dance present a creative improvisation using pillows (above and right) at a theatre in Ukraine, Europe. Younger students rehearse their interpretation of light (below).

Drama

Theatre Sports

Theatre sports are improvised games between individuals and teams of comedic performers. This form of drama develops many skills, including:

- quick thinking
- imagination
- creative role-play
- exploration of ideas.

ARTS FEATURE

The Genre of Comedy

A comedy is a form of entertainment that, in modern times, is intended to make us laugh. But comedy has taken many shapes throughout history. Originally, it referred to boisterous or rude songs that were sung by villagers at celebrations. In the times of the ancient Greeks and Romans, plays that ended happily were known as comedies.

Comedies in England

In England, by the sixteenth century, the term "comedies" had come to refer to light-hearted plays or stories where men and women overcame a series of disagreements, misunderstandings or blunders, and often ended up marrying each other despite their problems. Shakespeare wrote many comedies, such as *A Midsummer Night's Dream* and *All's Well That Ends Well.* In India, laughter has traditionally been recognised as one of the emotions that provides balance to the human spirit. Stories and plays translated from Sanskrit, an ancient Indian language, often deal with subjects designed to make people laugh.

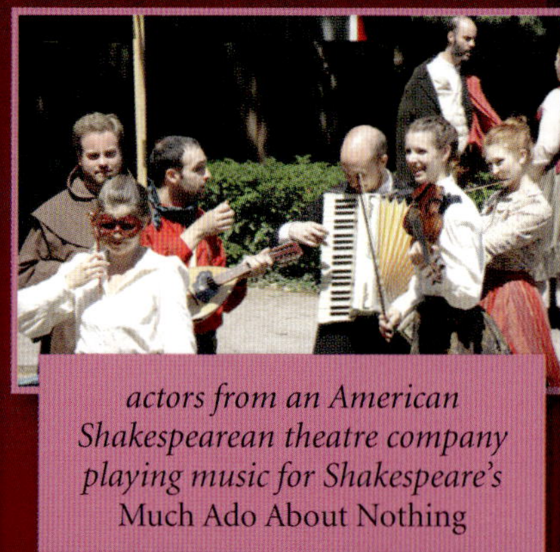

actors from an American Shakespearean theatre company playing music for Shakespeare's Much Ado About Nothing

The Many Guises of Comedy

In modern times, comedies often make people laugh because they exaggerate people's silly beliefs, sayings or behaviours. We find it humorous when people say or do something unexpected or absurd, and so comedies often feature people who are larger than life and who react to things differently than most people. Comedies may also reflect real-life situations in a way that makes us realise that sometimes the things we take seriously are really not that important.

4 How to Adapt Comedy Writing for Performance

TEXT TYPE
Procedure

Goal

To turn a funny story into a script for a comedy performance.

Materials

You will need a piece of humorous writing that takes place in a single location, has lots of dialogue and involves a cast of hilarious characters. A good example is the following extract from *Pirate Ship Makeover*:

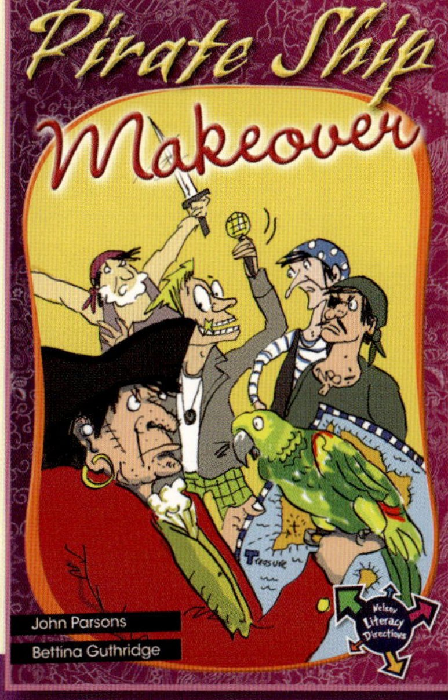

the cover for Pirate Ship Makeover, *which is one of the books available in the series Nelson Literacy Directions 6*

"Pirating sure ain't what it used to be," grumbled Captain Grizzlethorpe, reaching for the TV remote control. The disgruntled crew of the Charybdis *muttered and nodded their heads in resignation. Flotsam, the first mate, attempted a lacklustre ooh-arrgh, which turned into an embarrassing burp halfway through.*

"Pardon me," he murmured.

The crew of the Charybdis *had seen better days – and so had the cabin in which they sat. With its flickering TV screen, faded and moth-eaten comfortable chairs and half-eaten microwave dinners scattered around the deck, the* Charybdis *looked more like a weary retirement home for smelly buccaneers in need of a bath, than the fearsome scourge of the South Seas it had once been.*

Jawbones, the second mate, wriggled around in his chair uncomfortably. He screwed up his face and spat a microwaved pea out from the gap in his front teeth.

"Vegetables," he frowned, with a disgusted look. "Whatever happened to the good ol' days when dinners were just brown?"

"Aye, and they had browner gravy to hide the bits that weren't brown enough," agreed Flotsam with a sigh. "They were the good ol' days."

The rest of the pirates harrumphed and aarghed and rustled their cutlasses feebly in agreement. It had been quite a few years since any of them had woken up to a good ol' day.

The procedure continues on pages 16–19.

Steps

Step 1: Separate the dialogue from the descriptive writing, and start each character's dialogue on a new line, like this:

JAWBONES: Vegetables. Whatever happened to the good ol' days when dinners were just brown?

FLOTSAM: Aye, and they had browner gravy to hide the bits that weren't brown enough. They were the good ol' days.

Step 2: Add stage directions to the dialogue. These are instructions for the actors that will help them replicate what the characters in the story are doing. The actors will need to know when they should be frowning or smiling, or if they should be saying something with a mouthful of mashed potato!

CAPTAIN GRIZZLETHORPE: *(reaches for TV remote control)* Pirating sure ain't what it used to be.

FLOTSAM: *(looking sad and tired)* Ooh-arrgh. *(Burps loudly and looks embarrassed)* Pardon me!

Step 3: Make the script even funnier by writing in your own comedic touches. These could be audio or visual devices like expressions, pauses, noises and reactions. They could be unexpected, absurd, larger-than-life, or maybe a little bit rude – they just need to make people laugh!

CAPTAIN GRIZZLETHORPE: It's been quite a few years since any of us have woken up to a good ol' day.

(Entire cast nod their heads and roll their eyes in unison. As the curtain falls, Captain Grizzlethorpe turns in his chair again and, from behind the curtain, we hear a loud and embarrassing noise.)

CAPTAIN GRIZZLETHORPE: *(offstage)* Pardon!

The procedure continues on pages 18–19.

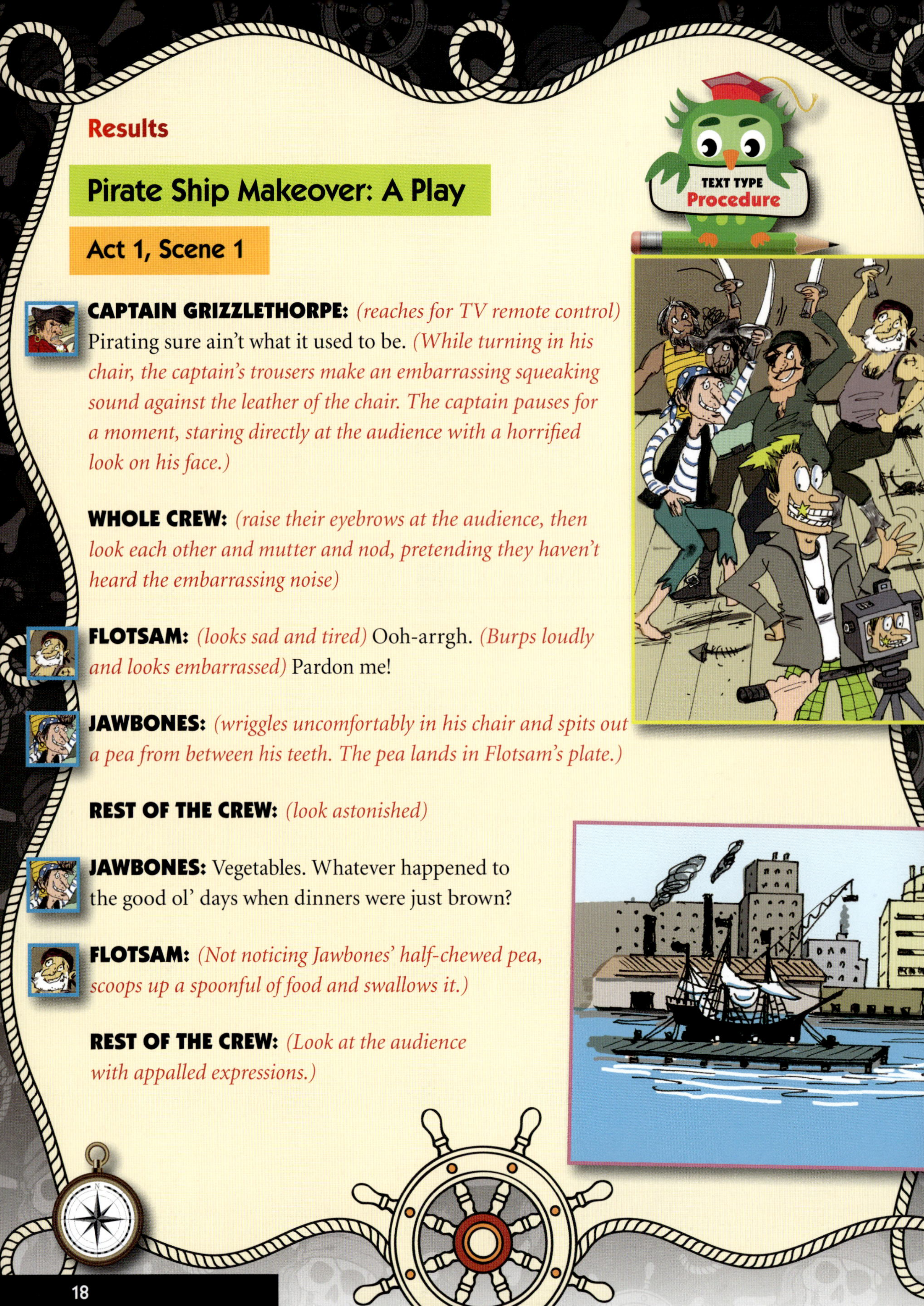

Results

Pirate Ship Makeover: A Play

Act 1, Scene 1

CAPTAIN GRIZZLETHORPE: *(reaches for TV remote control)* Pirating sure ain't what it used to be. *(While turning in his chair, the captain's trousers make an embarrassing squeaking sound against the leather of the chair. The captain pauses for a moment, staring directly at the audience with a horrified look on his face.)*

WHOLE CREW: *(raise their eyebrows at the audience, then look each other and mutter and nod, pretending they haven't heard the embarrassing noise)*

FLOTSAM: *(looks sad and tired)* Ooh-arrgh. *(Burps loudly and looks embarrassed)* Pardon me!

JAWBONES: *(wriggles uncomfortably in his chair and spits out a pea from between his teeth. The pea lands in Flotsam's plate.)*

REST OF THE CREW: *(look astonished)*

JAWBONES: Vegetables. Whatever happened to the good ol' days when dinners were just brown?

FLOTSAM: *(Not noticing Jawbones' half-chewed pea, scoops up a spoonful of food and swallows it.)*

REST OF THE CREW: *(Look at the audience with appalled expressions.)*

FLOTSAM: Aye, and they had browner gravy to hide the bits that weren't brown enough. They were the good ol' days.

REST OF THE CREW: *(push their plates away, clearly put off their dinners by the embarrassing sounds emanating from the captain's chair and the sight of Jawbones's spat-out food being eaten by Flotsam)* Ooh-arrgh, ooh-arrgh.

CAPTAIN GRIZZLETHORPE: It's been quite a few years since any of us have woken up to a good ol' day.

REST OF THE CREW: *(nod heads and roll their eyes in unison)*

(Curtain falls. From behind the curtain, we hear a loud and embarrassing noise.)

CAPTAIN GRIZZLETHORPE: *(offstage)* Pardon!

5 Performing a Musical Comedy

Queen Genevieve and the Soppy Songs

Queen Genevieve and the Soppy Songs is a humorous recount that uses both prose and song to bring the characters to life. The author was inspired by television talent shows where people perform songs in front of a panel of judges, and are either devastated or thrilled when the judges make their decisions.

The cover for Queen Genevieve and the Soppy Songs, *which is one of the books available in the series Nelson Literacy Directions 6.*

Adaptation of the Story Into a Play

An adaptation of the story centred around the songs could be a fun way to create a musical comedy that tells how Queen Genevieve chose a husband. The entire class could be involved in the following scene, using the songs from chapters 3 and 4 of the story.

SCENE: THE ROYAL PALACE OF QUEEN GENEVIEVE

CHARACTERS:
QUEEN GENEVIEVE
HOPEFUL SINGERS 1, 2, 3 (well-dressed suitors)
HOPEFUL SINGER 4 (a rough-looking farmer)
JUDGES 1, 2 and 3
AN ENTHUSIASTIC AUDIENCE

QUEEN GENEVIEVE:
Welcome to round one of my royal talent quest, where one of the four hopefuls on tonight's show will win the rather excellent prize of becoming my husband and also co-owner of my mince pie factory. Here are the rules. Each contestant will sing a song about how wonderful I am, and how extra-specially fantastic they would be as a husband. Based on the audience reaction, the judges' scoring, and whether or not I think they've captured my superbly gracious personality, I shall make my choice.

(*The* HOPEFUL SINGERS *and the* JUDGES *nod. The* ENTHUSIASTIC AUDIENCE *claps and cheers.*)

The Soppy Songs Competition Begins

JUDGES 1, 2 and 3: *(together)*
Hopeful Singer 1, the stage is yours.
Sing your song!

HOPEFUL SINGER 1:
(moves centre stage and bows)
Oh beauteous Genevieve,
how my knees quake!
My love for you
makes my fair heart ache.
I care not for your titles,
your riches, your pies.
It is simply your hand
for which my heart sighs.
With nary a gemstone,
no silver, nor gold,
My love will endure until we are old.
A smile or a wink
or a blush on your cheek,
These are the treasures, the riches I seek.
The minciest pie, the mushiest pea,
You are, Genevieve, these things to me.
You'll be my crumbliest pastry,
my tastiest sauce.
Assuming, of course, we do not divorce.

ENTHUSIASTIC AUDIENCE:
(claps and cheers)
Hooray!

JUDGES 1, 2 and 3: *(together)*
Hopeful Singer 2, the stage is yours.
Sing your song!

HOPEFUL SINGER 2:
(moves centre stage and bows)
O dearest queen,
listen well to my song.
Without this advice,
you might well choose wrong.
Pick not a scoundrel, rogue or vagabond!
For 'tis not your money, pies or castle
of which I'm fond.
I'll run my fingers through your hair,
not your gold.
I wish not for castles nor profit
from the pies you've sold.
All I crave is your sweet, gentle kiss.
Without it, I'll deflate
with a low, mournful hiss.
I'm thus afflicted, but easily cured.
One kiss and you'll banish
what I've long endured.
A kiss, my queen, to calm
this fluttering heart.
A kiss, my queen, to soothe Cupid's dart!

ENTHUSIASTIC AUDIENCE:
(claps and cheers)
Hooray!

The play continues on pages 22–23.

The Soppy Songs Competition Continues

JUDGES 1, 2 and 3: *(together)*
Hopeful Singer 3, the stage is yours.
Sing your song!

HOPEFUL SINGER 3: *(moves centre stage and bows)*
My love for you, I profess,
knows no bounds.
Beside your conversation,
there are no sweeter sounds.
My ardour for you burns deeply and bright.
My heart beats for you,
each long day and night.
I care not for treasures,
nor pastry nor mince.
From the moment our eyes met,
and then ever since,
I've felt like a sachet
whose lid has been peeled.
My blood runs like tomato sauce
that's thickly congealed.
My candle of love has been wantonly lit.
My dear queen, I beg you,
do not extinguish it.
Like a moth to a flame, to you I am drawn.
I'm besotted by you,
I'm completely lovelorn!

ENTHUSIASTIC AUDIENCE:
(claps and cheers)
Hooray!

JUDGES 1, 2 and 3: *(together)*
Hopeful Singer 4, the stage is yours.
Sing your song!

HOPEFUL SINGER 4: *(moves centre stage and bows)*
O dearest queen,
be under no illusion.
Suffer not from misconception
or confusion.
I've naught to offer,
but hard work and toil.
I cannot plant false hope,
just seeds in my soil.
You scrub up quite well,
that much I will say.
But you'll not look the same
by the end of a day
spent shovelling muck
and cooking my dinner.
You'll end up exhausted
and probably thinner.
For with this new husband,
there comes a new life.
Not only as queen, but a farmer's wife.
It'll mean early starts and endless chores,
but at the end of the day,
what's mine will be yours.

ENTHUSIASTIC AUDIENCE:
(falls silent)
Gasp!

JUDGES 1, 2 and 3: *(together)*
Oh dear!

Queen Genevieve Announces the Winner!

QUEEN GENEVIEVE:
I'm speechless. Judges, write down your scores. Audience, what do you think?

ENTHUSIASTIC AUDIENCE:
(loudly, with whoops and whistles)
Number 1! Number 2! Number 3!

JUDGE 1:
Queen Genevieve, we've come to a verdict. Here's the envelope!

QUEEN GENEVIEVE:
(reads the envelope and gazes at the **ENTHUSIASTIC AUDIENCE**
There can only be one winner.
And I have made my decision.

(Shakes head at **ENTHUSIASTIC AUDIENCE** *and tears the Judges' envelope in half.)*

ENTHUSIASTIC AUDIENCE and **JUDGES:**
Murmur, murmur!

QUEEN GENEVIEVE:
Each one of my suitors has shown talent and shrewdness with lyrics and music. But only one has demonstrated nothing but honesty and responsibility to those that depend upon him. I introduce to you the man who shall from this moment be known as Prince ... Prince, er ...

HOPEFUL SINGER 4: *(whispering and hitching up his pants)*
Kevin. My name's Kevin.

QUEEN GENEVIEVE:
Prince Kevin!

(**ENTHUSIASTIC AUDIENCE, JUDGES and HOPEFUL SINGERS 1, 2 and 3** *look bewildered.* **HOPEFUL SINGER 4** *moves centre stage and takes* **QUEEN GENEVIEVE's** *hand. Together they bow and then they kiss. Wild applause and cheering breaks out from everyone on stage.)*

Writing a Script for a TV Advertisement

Advertisements try to persuade us to do something, such as buy a product or support an organisation. Television advertisements often do this by telling a story accompanied with visual images. Advertising on television is expensive, so most advertisements are between 15 and 30 seconds long.

the cover for Due for Destruction, *which is one of the books available in the series Nelson Literacy Directions 6*

Write and Perform a TV Advertisement for a Dog Shelter

In the book *Due for Destruction*, which is a dramatic short novel, the author tells the story of how three main characters – Brooke, Karl and Dog 51 – are brought together in the setting of a shelter for abandoned dogs.

The story could easily be used as the basis for three short and effective television advertisements to persuade viewers to support the work of the dog shelter. Each character could use their perspective as the basis for a persuasive 15-second advertisement.

Meet the Characters

Brooke

Karl

Dog 51

Dog 51's Advertisement Brief

Background and Character Description

Dog 51 is an abandoned dog that has been left at an animal shelter. Everyone thinks he is dangerous. A series of images of Dog 51, with a gruff voice-over, would give the impression that the dog is telling his story.

Perform Dog 51's Advertisement

Dog 51 might say something like this:

"*I've had a tough life. I don't know how I got here. I don't even have a name. But I do have one thing: a friend. She talks to me, brings me food and water, and remembers that once, even I was a cute and cuddly puppy. While I'm in this cage, I can't help my friend. But you can. You can support the work of the dog shelter by giving a donation, doing some voluntary work, or even giving one of us dogs a new home. Please help my friend help me. It would mean a lot to us both.*"

The advertisements continue on pages 26–27.

Karl's Advertisement Brief

Background and Character Description

Karl is Brooke's father, and he has just been released from prison. He doesn't have anywhere to live and is relatively unknown to his daughter, Brooke.

Perform Karl's Advertisement

Karl's voice-over could go something like this:

I know what it's like to be in a cage. I know what it's like when your life doesn't work out the way you expected. I also know that when you're feeling all alone and abandoned, the only thing that keeps you going is the hope that one day, that cage door will be opened, and you can make a new start. By supporting the work of the shelter for abandoned dogs, you can help to give these animals a new start. Everyone – and everything – deserves a second chance, don't you think?

Brooke's Advertisement Brief

Background and Character Description

Brooke works at the dog shelter. She is a kind person whose loneliness is alleviated by the company of the dogs she cares for. One night, Dog 51 saves her from a dangerous situation.

Perform Brooke's Advertisement

Brooke's advertisement could go something like this:

Most of the time, it's tough working at the dog shelter. The dogs I see coming in are often frightened, unhealthy and have sometimes been treated very badly. But when I see the look on the face of a dog that has just been chosen for a new home with a new family, it makes it all worthwhile. Please help us to save more dogs. Not only could you help provide abandoned dogs with food, care and shelter – you could help to bring a new family together.

Advertisements Remind and Persuade People

All of these advertisement scripts could effectively tell the story of the dog shelter and persuade people to help. Why not read *Due for Destruction* and see if there are other ways that you could create a television advertisement to help the dog shelter? You never know, perhaps you'll come up with an effective way to promote the work of animal shelters, which could lead to making a lifetime of difference to a dog and its new family!

Setting the Scene

Illustrator Colours the Story

When an illustrator creates illustrations for a book, one of the things they may think about is how to use light and shade in their illustrations. A good illustrator will know that the way they use lighting in their illustrations can help to create mood. They will use tones of light and shade to reflect and reinforce the descriptions that the author has used to portray the settings and emotions in the story.

the cover for La Boca Twilight, *which is one of the books available in the series Nelson Literacy Directions 6*

Light and Sound Directors

In a script for a stage performance, the playwright will often brief the lighting director on what stage lighting effects are needed to create the mood of the scene. A play's sound director may also add sound effects or background music to further enhance the mood.

Meet the Characters

Victor Ruiz

Señora Salguero

Eduardo

Señor Florida

The Book: *La Boca Twilight*

In the book *La Boca Twilight*, the author has set most of the action in a single location – the interior of a cafe called La Perla. Depending on the time of day and the way the characters are feeling, the lighting in the illustrations changes. This affects the way the reader perceives the events that occur in the cafe.

La Boca Twilight: Daytime Scene

When the author first describes the interior of La Perla on page 16 of *La Boca Twilight*, it is daytime, when the cafe's worn-out condition is exposed. However, the main character, Victor, thinks that it is a magical place.

He looked around at the faded carpets, the scuffed and battered furniture, the grimy chandeliers, and saw only a glorious history, a place that for generations of musicians, dancers and patrons had been radiant with the promise of beauty.

Stage Adaptation: Daytime Scene

In a stage adaptation of *La Boca Twilight*, the lighting director might start by using bright, harsh lights so the audience can clearly see the dilapidated condition of the cafe. To show that Victor does not see its grimy reality, the lighting director might slowly dim the lighting and use a deep-red spotlight focused on the stage to show the audience what the character is visualising. The sound director might add the distant sounds of an old-fashioned tango band, and the sounds of people laughing and talking. In this way, the audience can more easily imagine what the character is thinking.

The stage adaptation continues on pages 30–31.

La Boca Twilight: Evening Scene

In chapter three, the setting is still inside La Perla, but it is now evening. The author starts the chapter on page 18 with this description.

That night, the patrons of La Perla were subdued. Beneath the old chandeliers, the cafe took on a different ambience, shadows hiding the stains and faded interior. Like Victor, no one looked at the décor. Instead, they watched the stage.

Filled with customers, La Perla has taken on a completely different feel.

Stage Adaptation: Evening Scene

In a stage adaptation, using exactly the same set, the lighting director could use rich, dark colours and shadows to create a sumptuous atmosphere in contrast to the run-down one revealed by the earlier bright lighting. A sound director could add the noises of people laughing and talking, chairs scraping, cups and saucers clinking, and perhaps an upbeat tango tune to establish a feeling of lively activity.

La Boca Twilight: Morning Scene

Later in the book, there is a sad scene when one of the characters is taken to hospital. This scene, described on page 40, takes place in the morning.

Gently, he picked up Señora Salguero, cradled her in his massive arms and silently carried her back inside La Perla. In the grey morning, the lights of the ambulancia *cast an eerie blue glow through the cafe's dusty windows.*

Stage Adaptation: Morning Scene

A lighting director could bring this scene to life by using stage lights to create a grey, shadowy interior to La Perla. Flashing blue lights at the back of the stage may indicate to the audience there is an ambulance present somewhere offstage. The sound director might decide to have no background music or noise in order to reinforce the sadness that the audience might be feeling. Exactly the same set could be used as previously but, once again, the lighting and the sound (or lack of it) may be used to dramatically change people's feelings about what is going on.

On-Stage Action!

On stage, movement, action and dialogue are the responsibilities of the actors. But when these are combined with lighting and sound effects, the audience can be drawn into a mood or emotion. Because a stage performance can only use dialogue, and the audience cannot be explicitly told what the character is thinking or feeling, the descriptive elements must be portrayed through light and sound. A good performance doesn't need lots of different sets, but it does help to have different lighting and sound effects.

Index

Glossary

lighting director A person who creates the lighting and atmosphere for a play, movie or television show

manuscript A book, document or other composition, written by an author

muse A source of inspiration or, in Greek mythology, any of the nine daughters of Mnemosyne and Zeus

mythology A collection of stories about the origin and history of a certain group of people, often involving superhuman beings or gods and the creation of the world

playwright A person who writes plays, also known as a dramatist

satire A play or story that uses humour, irony or wit to expose human vices, foolish behaviour or stupidity

script The dialogue and stage directions of a play, movie or television show

sonnet A type of poem consisting of 14-line verses

sound director A person who creates the sound effects and music for a play, movie or television show

tragedy A play or story where the main character suffers a great misfortune resulting in extreme sorrow